The Dead Sea Squirrels Series

Squirreled Away
Boy Meets Squirrels
Nutty Study Buddies
Squirrelnapped!
Tree-mendous Trouble
Whirly Squirrelies

Tree-mendous Trouble

Mike Nawrocki

Illustrated by Luke Séguin-Magee

Tyndale House Publishers
Carol Stream, Illinois

Visit Tyndale's website for kids at tyndale.com/kids.

TYNDALE is a registered trademark of Tyndale House Publishers. The Tyndale Kids logo is a trademark of Tyndale House Publishers.

The Dead Sea Squirrels is a registered trademark of Michael L. Nawrocki.

Tree-mendous Trouble

Designed by Libby Dykstra

Edited by Sarah Rubio

Published in association with the literary agency of Brentwood Studios, 1550 McEwen, Suite 300 PNB 17, Franklin, TN 37067.

Tree-mendous Trouble is a work of fiction. Where real people, events, establishments, organizations, or locales appear, they are used fictitiously. All other elements of the novel are drawn from the author's imagination.

For manufacturing information regarding this product, please call 1-800-323-9400.

For information about special discounts for bulk purchases, please contact Tyndale House Publishers at csresponse@tyndale.com, or call 1-800-323-9400.

Library of Congress Cataloging-in-Publication Data
Names: Nawrocki, Michael, author. | Séguin Magee, Luke, illustrator.
Title: Tree-mendous trouble / Mike Nawrocki ; illustrations by Luke Seguin-Magee.
Other titles: Tremendous trouble
Description: Carol Stream, Illinois : Tyndale House Publishers, Inc., [2020] | Series: Dead sea squirrels | Summary: Because not everyone has the best intentions for Merle and Pearl, two ancient squirrels from the time of Jesus who wake up in the twenty-first century, Michael and his family set up a security system.
Identifiers: LCCN 2019023527 (print) | LCCN 2019023528 (ebook) |ISBN 9781496435149 (trade paperback) | ISBN 9781496435156 (kindle edition) | ISBN 9781496435163 (epub) | ISBN 9781496435170 (epub)
Subjects: CYAC: Squirrels—Fiction. | Christian life—Fiction.
Classification: LCC PZ7.N185 Tr 2020 (print) | LCC PZ7.N185 (ebook) | DDC [Fic]—dc23
LC record available at https://lccn.loc.gov/2019023527
LC ebook record available at https://lccn.loc.gov/2019023528

Printed in the United States of America

26   25   24   23   22   21   20
7   6   5   4   3   2   1

To Dan—

*A great agent and an even better
friend. Thank you for your vision,
humility, and encouragement.*

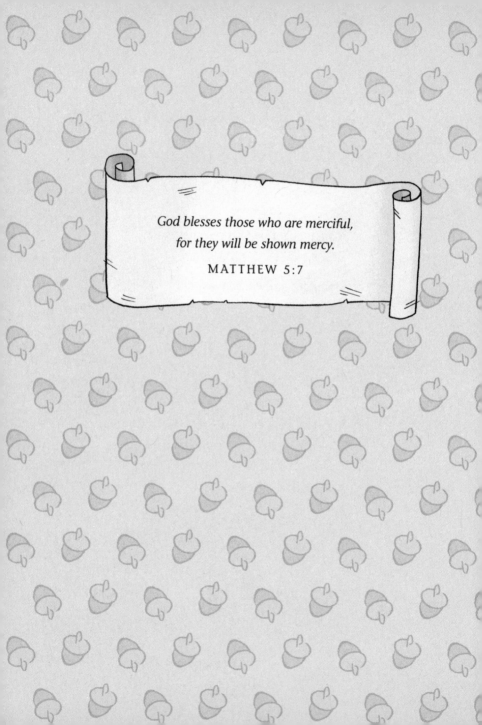

God blesses those who are merciful,
for they will be shown mercy.

MATTHEW 5:7

Ten-year-old Michael Gomez is spending the summer at the Dead Sea with his professor dad and his best friend, Justin.

While exploring a cave (without his dad's permission), Michael discovers two dried-out, salt-covered critters and stashes them in his backpack.

Michael sneaks the squirrels back home with him to Tennessee.

He sets them up like posable action figures on his dresser—under an open window.

While Michael is sleeping, a thunderstorm rolls in, and it begins to rain . . .

. . . rehydrating the squirrels!

Up and kicking again after almost 2,000 years, Merle and Pearl Squirrel have great stories and advice to share with the modern world.

They are the Dead Sea Squirrels!

CHAPTER 1

"It feels like the side of a boat," Pearl
Squirrel commented as she stroked the
wall of one of the rooms in the elabo-
rate hamster home Mrs. Gomez had
put together for Pearl and her husband, Merle. In her other paw, Pearl
held a tiny teacup Mrs. Gomez had
borrowed from one of her daughter,
Jane's, dolls. Jane had also come up
with a squirrel-sized fluffy pink robe
and a tiny pair of bunny slippers.
Pearl was getting some much-needed
pampering after being kidnapped by
and then rescued from the man in
the suit and sunglasses, a mysterious

agent working for a collector of ancient artifacts.

"It's called shiplap," Mrs. Gomez replied proudly as she and Jane sipped from their human-sized teacups. "Do you like it?"

"I love it!" Pearl gushed. "Feels so homey. Wooden walls are my favorite—just like a tree!"

"I'm so happy you like it!" Mrs. Gomez loved to decorate and was very excited for the chance to put a home

2

together for the two ancient squirrels her son, Michael, had accidentally adopted.

"Did you hear that, Merle?" Pearl called across the room to her husband, who was sitting with Dr. Gomez and Michael. "We've got shiplap!"

Merle had no idea what shiplap was but assumed it was a good thing and gave his wife a thumbs-up before returning to his conversation with Dr. Gomez and Michael. "Ever since I was a little pup, I'd wanted to see the Dead Sea," he said. "You can't sink!"

Dr. Gomez and Michael nodded, both having swum in the Dead Sea the previous summer. Dead Sea water is nearly 10 times saltier than the ocean. All that salt makes it impossible to sink.

"But how did you get there?" Dr. Gomez asked. As an anthropologist who had studied the area for years, he knew the Dead Sea was no place for tree squirrels. "And how did you get *here*? If we're going to keep you safe from the man in the suit and sunglasses, I need the full story."

Merle and Michael looked at each other. "Maybe you'd better sit down," Michael suggested, remembering how

his dad had fainted when he'd first heard Merle speak in his research lab at the university.

Dr. Gomez raised an eyebrow at his son but took a seat on the edge of Michael's bed. Then Merle and Michael told the story of how the squirrels had gotten to the Dead Sea in the 1st century and then to Walnut Creek, Tennessee, in the 21st. "It all started with the raft . . . ," Merle began.

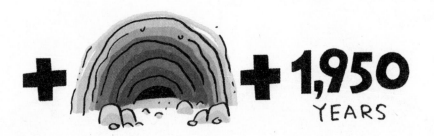

+ + 1,950 YEARS

CHAPTER 2

"Oh my," Dr. Gomez sighed.

"That's exactly what Mom said," Michael replied.

Dr. Gomez turned to look at his wife. "How long have you known?"

"Just since last night," Mrs. Gomez answered. "We had originally planned on telling you after you got home from work today."

"Well, this is huge." Dr. Gomez jumped up and started pacing the floor of Michael's bedroom. "There are a lot of people out there who will be interested in Merle and Pearl, and not all of them will have good intentions. We need to make sure the squirrels stay safe."

"I like the sound of that," Merle said. "Plus, it's not only people we have to worry about. Your kitty cat's intentions are also not that great." Merle was referring to Mr. Nemesis, the Gomez family's cat, who was not at all happy about having to share his house and people with a couple of ancient rodents. Since Merle and Pearl had arrived, Mr. Nemesis had spent a lot of time shut up in Jane's room.

"We'll need to install a security system," Dr. Gomez said. "I'll pick one up on Monday after work."

Michael liked the idea of a security system, but he was worried about the squirrels staying at home by themselves before it got put in. "Maybe I should take Merle and Pearl with me to school on Monday, since Mom and

Jane will be at school." Mrs. Gomez taught part-time at Jane's preschool.

"Yes!" Merle exclaimed. "Chicken nuggets!" Merle was fond of accompanying Michael to school, where this wonderful and exotic dish (to Merle) was a staple on the lunch menu. It even made up for having to stay crammed inside Michael's backpack most of the day.

"That's probably our best option, at least until the security system is up

and running," Dr. Gomez said. "I know I can't bring them to work. But be careful, and either Mom or I will need to drive you to school."

"We can't do this forever!" Michael said. "What are we going to do in the long run?"

Dr. Gomez sighed. "That's what I need to figure out."

CHAPTER 3

Monday morning, Michael, Jane, and the squirrels gathered around the table for breakfast before school.

"I've got something for you, Merle and Pearl!" Jane chirped, holding up two sets of tiny clothing. "Do you like them?"

"Um . . . what are they?" Merle asked, munching on an acorn.

"Outfits!" Jane replied.

"I think they're lovely," Pearl said. "Where did you get them?"

"From my dolls." Jane held the miniature dress up to Pearl. "I thought they would be good disguises and look cute on you."

Michael laughed so hard he nearly passed the hard-boiled egg he was eating through his nose. "Hrrrgh! Yeah, Merle! You'll look adorable!"

"I'm not putting that on!" Merle protested.

"You most certainly are!" Pearl crossed her paws. "It would be rude to not accept Jane's offer."

"Yeah, Merle! Ruuuuude!" Michael teased.

"Thank you, Jane," Pearl said, ignoring Michael. "This is very thoughtful of you."

Merle sighed. "Fine." He grabbed his outfit and disappeared behind a box of

Cocoa Fluffies to change. Jane handed
Pearl her outfit, and she joined her
husband behind the cereal box.

"Michael? Jane?" Mrs. Gomez called from the living room. "Are you finished with breakfast? We need to get going."

"Almost!" Michael responded, shoveling the last of his Cocoa Fluffies into his mouth.

"Jane, is Mr. Nemesis in your room? Did you shut the door?" Mrs. Gomez asked.

"Yes, Mama!" Jane responded. A faint cat yowl sounded from down the hall.

As Mrs. Gomez walked into the kitchen, Merle and Pearl stepped out from behind the cereal box, looking like squirrel versions of George and Martha Washington.

"Oh! Aren't you two adorable!"

Mrs. Gomez squealed, her voice almost drowned out by the sound of Michael's laughter.

CHAPTER 4

A narrow and shifty pair of cat eyes peered out of Jane's bedroom window as Mrs. Gomez pulled out of the driveway to take the kids and squirrels to school. You can tell how happy a dog is by how fast it wags its tail—the faster the wag, the happier the dog. It's the opposite for cats, and the speed of Mr. Nemesis's tail movements made it clear that this was one annoyed feline.

TAIL WAG SPEEDOMETER

CALM   ANNOYED

"Meeoooooowwwww!" Mr. Nemesis said, followed by a long string of other grouchy-sounding meows and growls. If you were to translate those sounds into English, they might have sounded something like a villain's monologue.

"I've had quite enough of those two overprivileged rodents," Mr. Nemesis groused. "'Oh, look at us. We're so old!'" he sneered. "'We're so cute! We speak human!' Big deal. I'm the widdle cutesy-puddie around here!"

Mr. Nemesis leaped from the windowsill over to Jane's bed, sinking deep into the coral-colored comforter. "And I'm not going to be cast aside, locked in this pink prison of fluff day and night while those squirrels roam freely around *my* house, stealing the affections of *my* family! It's a good

thing I'm just as brilliant as I am adorable," he remarked to Jane's stuffed
unicorn. "This nonsense is going to
stop—NOW."

With great effort, Mr. Nemesis
escaped the billowy down that encap-
sulated him, then hopped up onto
Jane's dresser. With a quick flick of
his tail, he set in motion a contrap-
tion that only an evil genius could
conceive of!

1.

2.

3.

4.

"Meooooowwwww," Mr. Nemesis purred (which, translated to English, means "HA HA HA HA! HAHAHA HAHA!") and jumped out the window.

CHAPTER 5

"Mmm, mmm, mmm!" Merle smacked his lips and licked his paws. He'd collected a few extra chicken nuggets at lunch.

"Shhhhh!" Pearl shushed him. The two were crammed inside Michael's backpack in Ms. McKay's class. "You're making too much noise! The teacher is going to hear you."

"Sorry. I can't help it," Merle whispered. Looking down, he discovered a chicken nugget crumb on the lapel of his George Washington jacket. "Hello there, little nugget-nugget! Didn't think you were going to get away, did you?"

"Shhhhh!" Pearl repeated.

Now that Merle was done eating, the prospect of three more hours in a backpack was starting to make him restless, and being dressed in doll clothes wasn't helping matters. He tugged at the waistband of his pants and scratched under his collar. "Maybe I could sneak outside and stretch my legs a bit?" he whispered.

Pearl vigorously shook her head.

"Take out your history books, please," Ms. McKay said. "Today we will be discussing the American Revolution." Michael reached inside his backpack and pulled out his history book. Since that was his largest book, it opened up a little more room for the squirrels.

"Thank you," Pearl said quietly to

Michael, who nodded as he opened his book on his desk.

Merle peeked out of the top of the backpack as the rest of the kids in the classroom dug in their backpacks for their books. At the front of the room, Ms. McKay was writing on the board with her back to the class. *It's now or never*, Merle decided. He sprang out of the backpack and made a break for the open window.

"Michael, would you—?" Ms. McKay stopped short in the middle of turning toward Michael, her eye caught by movement on the floor.

Merle, thinking fast, froze. He could sense he was being watched, and while a squirrel's first instinct is to run for the trees when spotted, Merle knew that it was not an option here.

"What is that?" Ms. McKay asked, staring at the motionless Merle.

"What is . . . what?" Michael asked nervously as Ms. McKay started over. "Um, it's . . . uh . . ."

The teacher reached down and picked up the revolutionary rodent. "Wow. He feels so real," Ms. McKay noted as Michael gulped hard. Merle had never tried so hard to stay so still in his life. "Michael," the teacher continued, "I am very impressed with your initiative!"

"My what?" Michael asked, still pale with fear.

"You dressed up your stuffed animal like George Washington for our lesson today! What is this—a squirrel? We'll call him 'George Washingsquirrel.'"

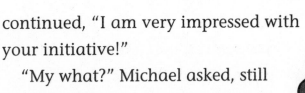

A ripple of laughter spread across the room. Michael sank low in his seat, his terror turning to sheer embarrassment.

"Do you mind if I set him on my desk for our lesson?" Ms. McKay asked. "He is just adorable."

The laughter got louder.

"No, ma'am," Michael muttered.

"Nice squirrel doll, Michael," Eric Weinstein teased. Michael shot him a quick grimace.

For the next 45 minutes, Merle was compelled to remain completely motionless atop Ms. McKay's desk as she talked about the Boston Tea Party.

"Serves him right," Pearl whispered to Michael. "I hope his whiskers itch."

CHAPTER 6

"Please don't eat us, sir!" Bob the Eastern gray squirrel pleaded. He was backed up against a tree trunk with his wife, Mary, and their friend Larry. Mr. Nemesis crouched on a branch in front of the trio, ready to pounce.

HOME
SWEET
HOME

"If we make a run for it, he can't catch us all!" Mary suggested nervously.

"Just the slowest one," Mr. Nemesis purred. The squirrels all looked at each other, wondering who might be the least speedy.

"If you let us go, I'll give you some nuts. I got extra," Larry bargained.

"Cats don't eat nuts, silly squirrel." Mr. Nemesis sharpened his claws on the branch, making the squirrels tremble. "But do you know what we *do* eat?"

"Umm . . . cat food?" Larry guessed.

"Oh yes, all kinds of cat food." Mr. Nemesis grinned. "Birds, mice . . . squirrels."

GULP. The three squirrels swallowed in unison.

Mr. Nemesis reached out with his
paw and pulled Larry closer to him.
"And squirrels are especially delicious."
He opened his mouth wide, showing
pointy white fangs.

"Larry!" Bob and Mary shouted in
horror.

"It's okay, guys," Larry cried, covering his eyes with his paws. "I was probably the slowest anyway."

Mr. Nemesis paused right before his teeth reached Larry. "You know, it doesn't have to go this way," he offered.

"You want to eat Bob instead?" Larry asked matter-of-factly.

"Larry!" Bob shouted, this time in annoyance.

"No, I don't need to eat any of you . . . if you cooperate," Mr. Nemesis said with a villainous grin.

"We love cooperating!" Mary blurted out.

"Yes!" Larry added. "Eastern gray squirrels are probably the cooperative-ist squirrels around."

"Most cooperative," Mr. Nemesis corrected.

"Yep! That's us!" Larry said.

"That's good to hear," Mr. Nemesis said. "So this is what's going to happen: you'll invite Merle and Pearl to your tree for dinner tonight, where I'll be waiting. Little will they know that *they'll* be the dinner!"

"Wait," Larry interrupted, a confused look on his face. "Why don't you just eat us? We're already caught."

Bob and Mary slapped their paws to their foreheads.

"Oh, it's not about dinner," Mr. Nemesis replied.

Bob and Mary sighed with relief.

"It's about revenge!"

CHAPTER 7

". . . and then around 100 men, some dressed as Mohawk warriors, boarded the *Dartmouth*, the *Eleanor*, and the *Beaver* and dumped all of the ships' 342 chests of tea into the water," Ms. McKay concluded. Merle, who had remained impressively frozen in place for nearly an hour, suddenly lost his balance and tumbled off the edge of the teacher's desk like a chest of tea into Boston Harbor, hitting the floor with a thud.

Michael sprang up from his seat. "I'll get that!" he announced, managing to cover up the sound of Merle's groan.

"Thanks for letting us borrow your squirrel, Michael!" Ms. McKay said as the bell rang.

"Yes, ma'am." Michael scooped Merle off the floor and stuffed him into his backpack, then hustled for the door with Justin.

"My whiskers itched sooooo bad!"
Merle complained as Michael, Justin,
Sadie, and the squirrels piled into Dr.
Gomez's car. Merle vigorously rubbed
his paws all over his snout, making up
for not being able to scratch earlier.

"I told you to stay put!" Pearl
laughed. "But you did look very dig-
nified up there, 'George Washingsquirrel'!"

The kids erupted into laughter as
Michael filled his dad in about Merle
getting caught by Ms. McKay.

"Guys, that is not funny," Dr. Gomez
said.

Merle shook his head in agreement.

"What would have happened if Ms.
McKay had figured out Merle wasn't
stuffed? That would have been a
disaster!"

"You're right, and Pearl was right. I should have stayed put. I'm very sorry," Merle said. "Next time, I'll stay in the backpack."

"Hopefully there won't be a next time," Dr. Gomez said. "I picked up the security system and will install it tonight. Merle and Pearl should be safe at home tomorrow."

"Oh, can I help?!" Merle asked. He loved tinkering with things, and installing something, whatever it was, sounded like fun to him. "I'm pretty good with my paws!"

"Sure, Merle," Dr. Gomez said. "I could use the help."

"Can Justin, Sadie, and I help too?" Michael asked.

"If you'll remember," Dr. Gomez said, "you're still grounded. I'm going to need to take Justin and Sadie home."

"Oh yeah," Michael said. He had broken his mom's favorite elephant-shaped end table by kicking a soccer ball in the house and then blamed it on his little sister. He was happy not to have been grounded for a year and didn't want to push his luck.

"But you can help Merle and me after we drop off your friends," his dad said.

"All right," Michael agreed.

"And when we're done, I have a call scheduled with Dr. Howard to figure out a long-term plan for the squirrels," Dr. Gomez added. Dr. Howard was Dad's boss at the university. Since Merle and Pearl had been discovered on the archaeological dig sponsored by the university, Dr. Gomez had an obligation to tell his boss about them.

"Dad!" Michael said, upset. "What if he wants to send Merle and Pearl back?! How's that any different from giving them to the man in the suit and sunglasses?"

Merle and Pearl exchanged a worried glance.

"I hope he doesn't," Dr. Gomez said. "But he needs to know."

CHAPTER 8

"How do I look, Mary?" Bob asked, flicking his tail.

"You clean up nice," Mary answered.

"Thank you. You do too," Bob replied. "We might just be the fanciest squirrels on the block!"

"What about me?" came their friend Larry's voice, sounding muffled.

"Quiet! You don't need to be fancy. You just need to stay put." Mr. Nemesis held his paw over a knothole in the walnut tree, trapping Larry inside. "You're my insurance that Bob and Mary will do what they're supposed to do."

"What are they supposed to do, again?" Larry asked from inside the tree.

Mr. Nemesis shook his head, annoyed. "For the 147th time, Bob and Mary will bring a gift to Merle and Pearl—"

Mary held up an acorn with a tiny red ribbon tied around it. "Got it!"

"—Bob and Mary will then invite

Merle and Pearl to dinner," Mr. Nemesis continued. "Bob! Line!"

Bob cleared his throat and recited, "Hello, neighbors. Mary and I would be delighted to have you over for dinner tonight. We have a special surprise for you. Please follow us."

43

"Ooh! What kind of surprise?!" Larry yelled from the hole.

"Me!" Mr. Nemesis shouted. "I'm the surprise!"

"They're not gonna like that!" Larry said.

Bob and Mary didn't like it either. The thought of tricking fellow squirrels, even if they were strangers, into a trap didn't sit right with them. But with their friend held hostage, they had little choice but to go along with the cat's plot.

"Oh, I suspect they won't." Mr. Nemesis grinned as his tail waved slowly back and forth. "But I'll be having squirrel for dinner tonight one way or the other. If not Merle and Pearl, then Larry here."

Larry squeaked with dismay. "Please hurry, Bob and Mary!"

CHAPTER 9

After dropping off Justin and Sadie,
Dr. Gomez and Michael returned
home with the squirrels to begin setting up the security system. Merle's
climbing abilities came in handy
for setting up sensors high on top of
doors and windows. Of course, first he
removed his George Washington outfit, which was quite cumbersome to
climb in.

"What do these things do?" Merle
wondered out loud as he attached a
sensor high on a wall.

"That one detects body heat. If
a person or animal comes into the
room, the sudden increase in infrared

47

energy sets off the alarm," Dr. Gomez explained.

"I have no idea what that means, but it sounds amazing," Merle said. "What about that one?" He pointed to another sensor on a window frame.

"That's a magnetic sensor," Dr. Gomez replied. "When a door or window is opened, it interrupts the magnetic field and sends an electric signal to the alarm."

"I'll take your word for it." Merle scratched his head. In the first century, the time period the squirrels had come from, infrared energy, magnetic fields, and electric signals had yet to be discovered.

Dr. Gomez and Merle finished setting up the sensors, then set the alarm from a panel in the kitchen. "All done," Dr. Gomez said, dusting off his hands. Merle offered him a fist bump, which he'd learned how to do from Sadie.

WOOO WOOO WOOO!

A brain-piercing sound rang out from every corner of the house. Merle and Pearl covered their ears with their paws.

"What is it?!!!" Pearl shouted.

"A window-vibration sensor in Michael's room has been tripped!" Dr. Gomez yelled over the alarm. Dr. Gomez, Michael, and the squirrels ran toward the bedroom. Opening the door, they spotted two gray squirrels standing on the windowsill: one was knocking on the closed window, and one was holding an acorn with a red bow on top.

"Well, the system works!" Dr. Gomez said. "Thankfully, these little gift-carrying critters look pretty harmless."

"Hello, neighbors," Bob the squirrel, speaking in squirrel, said as Michael slid the window open. "Mary and I would be delighted to have you over for dinner tonight." Mary nodded her head and smiled nervously.

"How lovely!" Pearl yelled over the alarm, still ringing in the background. "Please, come in."

Bob looked over his shoulder uneasily before completing his rehearsed line. "We have a special surprise for you. Please follow us."

"What are they saying?" Michael asked. He and Dr. Gomez didn't understand squirrel.

"They're inviting us over for dinner," Merle explained in a suspicious tone. A couple of days ago, he had gone out into the neighborhood to look for a tree home for himself and Pearl and had been met with less-than-welcoming attitudes from the neighborhood squirrels. He wondered why they would suddenly be so nice.

"You all have a nice visit," Dr. Gomez

said as he headed back toward the kitchen. "I need to reset the alarm and call Dr. Howard."

"Dad! Wait!!!" Michael pleaded, following after him.

CHAPTER 10

Meanwhile, Mr. Nemesis peeked
down from his perch in the walnut
tree, keeping an eye on Bob and Mary
through the open window below. The
cat's left paw rested over the knothole
in the tree, still holding Larry hostage.

"What's going on down there?"
Larry asked.

"Shhhhh!" Mr. Nemesis hushed him.
"I can't hear them with you talking."

Some fidgeting and scrabbling
sounds came from inside the tree.
"I really need to go to the bathroom,"
came Larry's voice. "Can you let me
out for a sec?"

"What?" Mr. Nemesis scowled. "Why don't you just go in the tree?"

"Excuse me?" Larry replied, insulted. "I'm not a barbarian. Do you use the bathroom inside your home?"

"As a matter of fact, I do," Mr. Nemesis said, recalling his litter box in the laundry room. "You're staying right where you are."

Most common squirrels don't have a problem with peeing in their trees, but Larry was a bit of a neat freak, and he wasn't about to start doing it now. "Please let me out!" he begged.

"Quiet!" the cat hissed.

If you've ever been in a place where you've really needed to go potty and couldn't, either because you were in a car stuck in traffic or in a department store where you couldn't find where the restrooms were hidden, you know how desperate Larry was starting to feel. "C'mon! It'll just take me a second!" Larry pleaded.

"You are not going anywhere."

Inside the tree, Larry looked around anxiously for possible alternate exits. Nothing. He could feel the sweat starting to bead on his forehead. He looked at the main exit, blocked by the soft, pink pads on Mr. Nemesis's paw. The cat was too strong for Larry to force his way through.

55

That's when he spotted it—a large, sharp splinter, about the size of a pencil, hanging off the side of his enclosure like a stalactite. *Desperate times call for desperate measures*, Larry thought as he snapped off the splinter. "I'm asking you one more time!" he called out.

"And I'm telling you *no* one more time," Mr. Nemesis replied.

"Okay," Larry said. "Sorry about this."

"Sorry about whAAAAAAAAAAAAAAA?!!!!!" The cat screamed as the splinter lanced his paw. Reeling backward, Mr. Nemesis lost his footing on the large branch where he stood. As his back claws slid off the branch, he tried to reach out with his front paws, but the stabbing pain from the splinter prevented him from being able to grab it.

He fell.

CHAPTER 11

Piercing feline screams interrupted Bob and Mary's welcome wagon. Merle, Pearl, and the Tennessee squirrels all turned quickly toward the ear-splitting sounds coming from the walnut tree outside Michael's window. Mr. Nemesis, with his right front paw held high, slipped off an upper branch and plummeted toward the ground.

They say that cats always land on their feet. This is because cats have something called a "righting reflex," which allows them to turn their bodies in midair to point their paws downward. In the middle of his righting reflex, Mr. Nemesis struck a branch and was instantly unrighted. He twisted violently around and struck another thin branch. This time, however, he was able to grab hold of the twig with his right front paw (the one without the splinter). Mr. Nemesis hung on for dear life, hissing up a storm.

"Larry!!! You okay???" Bob yelled frantically.

"Who's Larry?" Merle wondered.

"Hold on a sec." Larry's relieved voice sounded from high in the tree.

"Where are you?!" Mary called out.

"Hold on. Gimme a few." Then they heard a relieved-sounding sigh.

"What's going on?!" Bob demanded.

"Can you just hold your horses?!" Larry replied, annoyed.

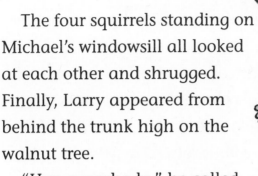

The four squirrels standing on Michael's windowsill all looked at each other and shrugged. Finally, Larry appeared from behind the trunk high on the walnut tree.

"Hey, everybody," he called down. "Feeling much better now." He spotted Mr. Nemesis holding on to the branch below. "Oh, hey, sorry about that, kitty. When you gotta go, you gotta go, am I right?"

Mr. Nemesis let out a loud, angry growl.

"What is happening here?"

Pearl demanded. "This all looks really fishy."

As the cat continued to dangle high in the air above them, Bob and Mary came clean about Mr. Nemesis's plot.

"Why, that rotten cat!" Merle exclaimed.

"We're so sorry we went along with it," Mary apologized. "But he was going to eat our friend."

"And he wouldn't even give me a potty break!" Larry added from on high.

Pearl gazed at the helpless, dangling feline. "We need to help him before he gets hurt."

Merle, Bob, and Mary turned toward Pearl.

they said in unison.

"We're not helping that cat!"
Merle exclaimed. "He was going
to eat us!"

"Are you nuts?!" Mary said.

"Merle," Pearl said calmly, "I think we need to show some mercy to Mr. Nemesis."

"Mercy?! Mercy?!" Merle repeated. "Why in the world would we do that?!"

BEST WALNUTS in the HOLY LAND

CHAPTER 12

SQUIRREL'S-EYE VIEW

"Merle, do you remember the story we told Michael this weekend from the Sea of Galilee?" Pearl asked.

"I sure do! Finest walnuts in the Holy Land!" Merle replied, recalling the time he and Pearl had been gathering food by the shore of the sea and found themselves at the Sermon on the Mount. "'Do to others whatever you would like them to do to you.'"

"Good. I'm glad you remember," Pearl answered.

"That's something the cat should have thought about," Merle said, crossing his paws. "If he wants help from squirrels, he should avoid trying to eat them." He called up to Mr. Nemesis, "DO TO OTHERS, MR. CAT! AM I RIGHT?!"

Mr. Nemesis replied with a loud hiss.

"I'm referring to the part just before that," Pearl said calmly. "The blessings."

"Jesus said, 'God blesses those who are merciful, for they will be shown mercy,'" recalled Pearl. Merle and Pearl had sat high up in a tree, watching Jesus teach a very large crowd of people. "It was one of Jesus' eight blessings, or beatitudes. The first three blessings are for those who know they need God, that they aren't good enough or strong enough by themselves. They realize they are empty and need God to fill them up!"

God blesses those who are poor and realize their need for him, for the Kingdom of Heaven is theirs.

God blesses those who mourn, for they will be comforted.

God blesses those who are humble, for they will inherit the whole earth.

Pearl continued, "When we realize how much we need God and let him fill us up, we want to be more like him. We start to want it as much as we want food and water when we're hungry or thirsty."

God blesses those who hunger and thirst for justice, for they will be satisfied.

67

"And the next three blessings come when we are more like God," Pearl said.

God blesses those who are merciful, for they will be shown mercy.

God blesses those whose hearts are pure, for they will see God.

God blesses those who work for peace, for they will be called the children of God.

"That's quite a memory you've got there, Pearl," Bob admitted. "Even for a squirrel!"

CHAPTER 13

"So, when we are merciful, we're acting more like God?" Mary asked.

"Exactly!" Pearl replied. "We can be merciful to others because God has been merciful to us."

"Even our enemies?" Bob asked.

"Especially our enemies," Pearl said.

"Even Mr. Nemesis?" Mary watched the fierce feline, still dangling from the branch by one claw.

"I suppose since *nemesis* actually means 'enemy,' he would be included," Pearl confirmed.

"Well, there is no way I'm helping him!" Merle exclaimed, stepping back from the window. "He'll eat us the first chance he gets." Bob and Mary sided with Merle, leaving Pearl standing alone.

"Fine," Pearl said. "If you won't help him, I will. I'll go and get Michael. Hold on!" Pearl called up to the cat, "I'm going to get help!"

"Michael won't want to help him either!" Merle said.

"Then I'll get Jane." Pearl scurried out into the hallway to find the little girl, just as Larry hopped through the window from the walnut tree to join the others.

"Jane will definitely help," Merle said.
"She loves Mr. Nemesis." He shrugged.
"Who knows why."

"Hey?!" Bob asked, holding up his
two front paws. He had been counting
beatitudes with his toes. "I only counted
seven." Since squirrels have only a total
of eight toes on their front paws, he was

almost out of toes. He stuck up his last one. "What about number eight?"

"God blesses those who are persecuted for doing right," Merle recalled.

"Oh, great," Larry said. "If Pearl gets Mr. Nemesis down from that tree, prepare to be blessed."

CHAPTER 14

"Is this some kind of joke, Gomez?!"
Dr. Howard barked into the phone.
Dr. Gomez could hear a roar in the
background that he guessed must be
the powerful engine of Dr. Howard's
convertible. "You have urgent information regarding squirrels? It's been
a long day—this better be good." Dr.
Howard seldom went on digs or taught
classes like the professors who worked
for him, but he always seemed to be
very busy—usually on his way to very
important lunches and dinners.

"No, Dr. Howard, this is not a joke."
Dr. Gomez was in his home office,
Michael hanging over his shoulder,

trying to listen in. "I'm in possession of two ancient squirrels from the Dead Sea."

"Dad, please!" Michael whispered.

"Actually, sir, let me restate that," Dr. Gomez said, waving at Michael to be quiet. "They were found near the Dead Sea dig, but they're actually from somewhere north of the sea. They were vacationing there and got stuck."

"Vacationing???" Dr. Howard shouted over the sound of tires squealing. Dr. Gomez imagined him rolling his eyes as he cruised down a winding road. "Vacationing squirrels, right. And how did you gather this information from these . . . squirrels?"

"They, ah . . . they told me," Dr. Gomez answered uncomfortably.

A long pause followed. Dr. Gomez listened to the sound of rushing wind over the phone. Finally Dr. Howard said, "So, these squirrels, they . . . talk, do they?"

"Yes, sir." Dr. Gomez covered his face with one hand.

Michael sighed deeply and shook his head. There was no turning back now.

"Aramaic, no doubt?" Dr. Howard mocked. "Or perhaps Hebrew, or maybe even Latin?"

"Well, they may also speak those languages. And squirrel, of course, 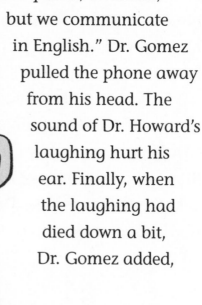 but we communicate in English." Dr. Gomez pulled the phone away from his head. The sound of Dr. Howard's laughing hurt his ear. Finally, when the laughing had died down a bit, Dr. Gomez added,

76

"Sir, if you don't believe me, you should come see for yourself."

Michael threw his hands up in the air. "This is terrible!"

"Shhhhh!" Dr. Gomez shushed.

"Am I being shushed?" Dr. Howard shouted.

"Sorry, sir. I wasn't shushing you," Dr. Gomez said.

"Okay, Gomez," Dr. Howard said, honking his horn. "Let's see if you can make more sense in person. I'll be at your place in five, if this slowpoke gets out of my way." He laid on the horn again.

"All right, sir. Thank you." Dr. Gomez hung up the phone and informed his very unhappy son, "He'll be here soon."

CHAPTER 15

While Dr. Gomez wrapped up the call
with his boss, Pearl ran to Jane's room.
The little girl was re-dressing her dolls
in the George and Martha Washington
clothes the squirrels had worn to
school.

"Jane! Mr. Nemesis needs help—he's
stuck!" Pearl gasped, leaping up onto
the windowsill.

Jane dropped her dolls and hurried
to her window. Following the direction
of Pearl's gaze, she saw Mr. Nemesis
hanging perilously from the tree like
a frightened monkey. Jane opened her
window to call out to her cat, setting
off the burglar alarm.

WOOO WOOO WOOO!!!

"I'm coming, Mr. Nemesis!" Jane shouted over the shrieking alarm. "Hang on!!!"

Michael, in Dr. Gomez's office, jumped as the alarm sounded. "Again?!" He took off running toward his room, his dad close behind.

"Help!" they heard Jane yell as they passed her doorway. Dr. Gomez ducked into Jane's room, followed by Michael, and joined his daughter and Pearl at the window.

"Why is Mr. Nemesis up in the tree?"
Michael wondered.

"It was part of his plan to eat us," Merle said, joining the crowd around the window.

"I say leave him up there, then!" Michael yelled.

Merle turned to Pearl and shrugged. "What did I tell you?"

"I know, but we've got to help save that poor cat anyway," Pearl said.

Dr. Gomez gave everyone their orders, the alarm still blaring in the background. "Michael, you and Merle go to the garage and get my ladder. Jane, you and Pearl follow them and grab my fishing net. Meet me by the tree."

The kids and squirrels headed to the garage, while Dr. Gomez ran outside, disarming the alarm on his way.

Unlike squirrels, who, as you may

recall, have just four toes and claws on their front paws, cats have five. Which was very fortunate indeed for Mr. Nemesis. Losing strength and slipping, he was now hanging onto the branch with his fifth and final claw!

CHAPTER 16

Dr. Gomez stood directly under
Mr. Nemesis to try to break the cat's fall
in case he dropped before the rescue
equipment arrived. However, Dr. Gomez
was very nervous about the fact that he
was wearing a short-sleeved shirt. If he
had to catch a falling cat with his bare
arms, he was sure to end up looking
like he'd wrestled a rosebush. "Hurry!"
he called to Michael and Jane as they
exited the garage with the ladder
and fishing net.

Michael set up the ladder as Jane
handed her dad the net. Dr. Gomez
climbed to the top rung of the ladder
as Michael, Merle, and Pearl held it

steady at its base. The Tennessee squirrels remained on Michael's windowsill,
nervously watching the action, while
Jane stood in the yard and cried.

"Poor Mr. Nemesis! Hang on!" she
wailed.

Dr. Gomez extended the net as high
up as he could, but it was still a couple
of feet under the cat.

"Climb up higher!" Jane cried. "He's
scared!"

"Meow!!!" Mr. Nemesis howled in
confirmation.

"It's not a step! It's not a step!"
Dr. Gomez yelled, reading the warning printed on the top of every A-frame
ladder. "C'mon, Mr. Nemesis! Let go!
I'll catch you!"

"MEOW!!!" the cat howled
even louder.

"I'll help!" Larry the squirrel offered. He jumped onto the tree trunk and scurried up into the branches.

"Mr. Nemesis, let go!" Dr. Gomez repeated.

Larry took hold of the branch the desperate cat was clinging to and began shaking it wildly.

"What are you doing?!!!" Mr. Nemesis demanded. To Dr. Gomez and the kids, it just sounded like a howl.

"Just being neigh-borly!" Larry yelled, stomping on the thin branch with all his weight. Suddenly,

the twig snapped! Larry was able to grab on to a nearby branch as Mr. Nemesis fell safely into the waiting fishing net.

"Hurray!" Jane shouted. Her precious kitty was now safe in the netting, though squirming wildly and making sounds seldom heard from a cat.

"I'll get all of you! You'll all be sorry!" Merle, Pearl, Bob, Mary, and Larry heard Mr. Nemesis scream as

Jane removed him from the net and took him back inside. He tried to break free and come after the squirrels, but the little girl's loving embrace was too tight. Before he knew it, Mr. Nemesis was purring helplessly as Jane scratched him behind his ears.

"Poor baby kitty—flying through the air like a big butterfly," Jane cooed as Mr. Nemesis glared at the squirrels over her shoulder.

"You see, Pearl! You helped him out, and now he's going to get us! Where's the blessing in that?!" Merle asked.

"Merle, showing mercy to others isn't about being sure they'll be merciful to us in return. We do it because God was first merciful to us," Pearl explained. "We don't deserve the mercy he gives. It's a gift that he gives that we should also give to others, whether they deserve it or not."

Merle, Bob, Mary, and Larry thought about Pearl's words. "Who knows?" Bob said. "Maybe one day Mr. Nemesis will come to realize the same thing."

Dr. Gomez looked down at Bob, who to his ears was squeaking wildly. "Did that squirrel just say something?" he asked Merle.

CHAPTER 17

"I hope it's not too late to accept
your dinner invitation," Pearl said to
Bob and Mary. "That is, if you're still
offering it."

"Of course!" Mary said. "And again,
we are so sorry about going along with
the cat's plan."

"We were just trying to save our
buddy Larry," Bob explained.

"I get it," Merle replied. "No hard
feelings. It'll be good to get to know
you!"

"Merle and I will go freshen up and
be right with you," Pearl said.

"I don't really freshen up," Merle
pointed out.

"Well, I need to, and you're coming with me." Pearl took Merle by the paw and headed back into the house.

Just as they hopped through Michael's bedroom window, a neon-blue convertible with a spoiler and low-profile tires rolled up into the Gomezes' driveway. Michael and his dad walked over to it, Bob and Mary following behind. "All right, Gomez," Dr. Howard shouted through his window, not bothering to get out of the car. "Let's hear from these amazing Dead Sea squirrels."

"Oh, they just went into the house to freshen up," Mary the squirrel said. But all Dr. Howard, Dr. Gomez, and Michael heard was, "Squeak, squeak . . . squeak, squeak, squeak."

Bob followed up with, "You'll love meeting them. Maybe we could all have dinner together?"

"Do you like nuts?" Larry asked from the tree.

Bob and Larry's voices also only sounded like cute squirrel squeaks to the assembled humans.

Dr. Howard shook his head. "Yep. That's what I thought," he muttered.

"Sir, these aren't—" Dr. Gomez tried to explain, but Dr. Howard cut him off.

"Look, Gomez," he said gruffly. "You spent all summer under the hot sun. Maybe you forgot to wear a hat?"

"No, I promise you—" Dr. Gomez stammered.

"Take the rest of the week off," Dr. Howard offered, putting the car in reverse. "Rest up. Keep out of the sun. I'll get Esteban to cover for you." He backed out of the driveway and took off, tires screeching.

Michael waved goodbye to his
dad's boss, a relieved grin on his face.
"Thanks for coming, Dr. Howard! I'll
make sure Dad stays hydrated!"

CHAPTER 18

Knock, knock, knock, Michael heard on his window. It was now dark out, and Merle and Pearl were returning from their evening with the Tennessee squirrels.

"How did it go?" Michael asked as he slid open his window for his friends to enter.

"Just lovely," Pearl responded. "It's nice to get to know some local squirrels."

"That Larry is a kook," Merle said. "Loads of fun!"

Now that everyone was safe inside for the evening, Michael let his dad know he could arm the alarm. *Boop, boop*, they heard from the kitchen.

Michael filled the squirrels in on Dr. Howard's visit. "So, my dad's boss thought Bob and Mary were you guys!" he laughed. "I don't think we'll need to worry about the university sending you back now."

"Phew! That's a relief!" Merle exclaimed. He and Pearl settled into their huge modified hamster house that Michael's mom had put together for them. "Now all we have to worry about is that cat!"

"It was very nice of you guys to help Mr. Nemesis," Michael said. "It was the right thing to do."

"You're right," Merle said. "I just hope it doesn't come back to bite us . . . literally."

The friends had a good laugh as they settled in for sleep, Michael in his bed and Merle and Pearl in their cozy sawdust. It had been a very busy day for all of them, so it wasn't long before they all drifted off.

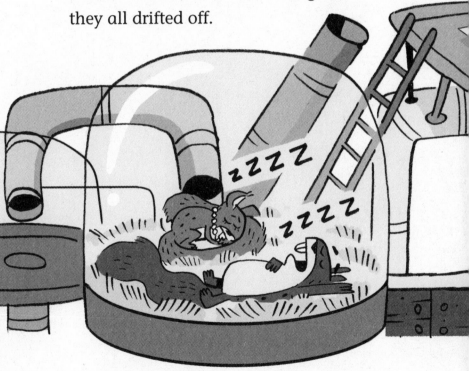

And that's when the alarm went off!

MICHAEL GOMEZ is an adventurous and active 10-year-old boy. He is kindhearted but often acts before he thinks. He's friendly and talkative and blissfully unaware that most of his classmates think he's a bit geeky. Michael is super excited to be in fifth grade, which, in his mind, makes him "grade school royalty!"

MERLE SQUIRREL may be thousands of years old, but he never really grew up. He has endless enthusiasm for anything new and interesting—especially this strange modern world he finds himself in. He marvels at the self-refilling bowl of fresh drinking water (otherwise known as a toilet) and supplements his regular diet of tree nuts with what he believes might be the world's most perfect food: chicken nuggets. He's old enough to know better, but he often finds it hard to do better. Good thing he's got his wife, Pearl, to help him make wise choices.

PEARL SQUIRREL is wise beyond her many, many, many years, with enough common sense for both her and Merle. When Michael's in a bind, she loves to share a lesson or bit of wisdom from Bible events she witnessed in her youth. Pearl's biggest quirk is that she is a nut hoarder. Having come from a world where food is scarce, her instinct is to grab whatever she can. The abundance and variety of nuts in present-day Tennessee can lead to distraction and storage issues.

JUSTIN KESSLER is Michael's best friend. Justin is quieter and has better judgment than Michael, and he is super smart. He's a rule follower and is obsessed with being on time. He'll usually give in to what Michael wants to do after warning him of the likely consequences.

SADIE HENDERSON is Michael and Justin's other best friend. She enjoys video games and bowling just as much as cheerleading and pajama parties. She gets mad respect from her classmates as the only kid at Walnut Creek Elementary who's not afraid of school bully Edgar. Though Sadie's in a different homeroom than her two best friends, the three always sit together at lunch and hang out after class.

DR. GOMEZ, a professor of anthropology, is not thrilled when he finds out that his son, Michael, smuggled two ancient squirrels home from their summer trip to the Dead Sea, but he ends up seeing great value in having them around as original sources for his research. Dad loves his son's adventurous spirit but wishes Michael would look (or at least peek) before he leaps.

MRS. GOMEZ teaches part-time at her daughter's preschool and is a full-time mom to Michael and Jane. She feels sorry for the fish-out-of-water squirrels and looks for ways to help them feel at home, including constructing and decorating an over-the-top hamster mansion for Merle and Pearl in Michael's room. She also can't help but call Michael by her favorite (and his least favorite) nickname, Cookies.

MR. NEMESIS is the Gomez family cat who becomes Merle and Pearl's true nemesis. Jealous of the time and attention given to the squirrels by his family, Mr. Nemesis is continuously coming up with brilliant and creative ways to get rid of them. He hides his ability to talk from the family, but not the squirrels.

JANE GOMEZ is Michael's little sister. She's super adorable but delights in getting her brother busted so she can be known as the "good child." She thinks Merle and Pearl are the cutest things she has ever seen in her whole life (next to Mr. Nemesis) and is fond of dressing them up in her doll clothes.

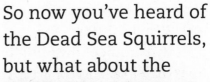

DR. GOMEZ'S
Historical Handbook

So now you've heard of the Dead Sea Squirrels, but what about the **DEAD SEA *SCROLLS*?**

Way back in 1946, just after the end of World War II, in a cave along the banks of the Dead Sea, a 15-year-old boy came across some jars containing ancient scrolls while looking after his goats. When scholars and archaeologists found out about his discovery, the hunt for more scrolls was on! Over the next 10 years, many more scrolls and pieces of scrolls were found in 11 different caves.

There are different theories about exactly who wrote on the scrolls and hid them in the caves. One of the most popular ideas is that they belonged to a group of Jewish priests called Essenes, who lived in the desert because they had been thrown out of Jerusalem. One thing is for sure—the scrolls are very, very old! They were placed in the caves between the years 300 BC and AD 100!

Forty percent of the words on the scrolls come from the Bible. Parts of every Old Testament book except for the book of Esther have been discovered.

Of the remaining 60 percent, half are religious texts not found in the Bible, and half are historical records about the way people lived 2,000 years ago.

The discovery of the Dead Sea Scrolls is one of the most important archaeological finds in history!

About the Author

As co-creator of VeggieTales, co-founder of Big Idea Entertainment, and the voice of the beloved Larry the Cucumber, **MIKE NAWROCKI** has been dedicated to helping parents pass on biblical values to their kids through storytelling for over two decades. Mike currently serves as Assistant Professor of Film and Animation at Lipscomb University in Nashville, Tennessee, and makes his home in nearby Franklin with his wife, Lisa, and their two children. The Dead Sea Squirrels is Mike's first children's book series.

You'll have to read
Whirly Squirrelies
to find out!